This **PJ BOOK** belongs to

PJ Library®

JEWISH BEDTIME STORIES and SONGS

Passover Terms

AFIKOMAN: Meaning "dessert," it is a piece of matzoh broken near the beginning of the seder and put aside to be eaten at the end of the meal. Traditionally, children "steal" the afikoman and then ransom it for gifts when the meal is finished.

HAGGADAH: Meaning "telling," it is the book of prayers, Bible verses, and explanations that tells the story of slavery in Egypt and offers thanks for freedom; it also explains the order of the Passover seder. The Haggadah is probably the most frequently printed Jewish text of all time, and many families use beautifully illustrated Haggadahs.

MATZOH: Unleavened bread, or bread that has not fermented and risen, made with only flour and water, quickly cooked, and flat. It is the only kind of bread permitted on Passover.

PASSOVER: A weeklong festival, celebrated in the spring, commemorating the exodus of the Jews from Egypt. No leaven (such as made with yeast or sourdough) can be kept or eaten during the length of the festival. The beginning of the holiday is marked with the seder.

SEDER: Meaning "order" or "arrangement," the seder is the feast held at the beginning of Passover. It follows a specific order of readings and rituals and can go on for many hours.

the Yankee at the Seder

By Elka Weber   Illustrations by Adam Gustavson

TRICYCLE PRESS
Berkeley

Acknowledgments

Many thanks to Myer Levy's great-granddaughter Judith McLaughlin,
who graciously got in touch with me, and to her son-in-law Jason Wagner.
Both were generous about sharing their family's part in history.

Thanks also to the Mikveh Israel Archive and the Congregation Mikveh Israel of
Philadelphia, for providing information about the life and background of Myer Levy.

The publisher is grateful to Deborah Brodie and historian Jeffrey Greenhut, PhD,
for their expert and careful review of this book.

Text copyright © 2009 by Elka Weber
Cover art and interior illustrations copyright © 2009
by Adam Gustavson

All rights reserved. Published in the United States by
Tricycle Press, an imprint of Random House Children's Books,
a division of Penguin Random House LLC, New York.

rhcbooks.com

Tricycle Press and the colophon are registered trademarks of Penguin
Random House LLC.

Picture Credits: Joseph and Rachel Levy and Civil War–era Haggadah,
from the archives of Congregation Mikveh Israel of Philadelphia,
Miss Miriam E. Levy Collection; Myer Levy's saber, courtesy of
Judith McLaughlin, photographed by Jason Wagner; photograph
of Myer Levy and his wife, courtesy of Judith McLaughlin.

Library of Congress Cataloging-in-Publication Data
Weber, Elka, 1968–
The Yankee at the seder / by Elka Weber ; illustrations by
Adam Gustavson.
p. cm.
Summary: As a Confederate family prepares for Passover the day after
the Civil War has ended, a Yankee arrives on their Virginia doorstep
and is invited to share their meal, to the dismay of ten-year-old Jacob.
Includes historical notes about Corporal Myer Levy, on whom the
story is based, and his prominent Philadelphia family.
ISBN 978-1-58246-256-1 (hardcover)
[1. Passover—Fiction. 2. Seder—Fiction. 3. Jews—United States—
Fiction. 4. Soldiers—Fiction. 5. Virginia—History—Civil War,
1861–1865—Fiction.]
I. Gustavson, Adam, ill. II. Title.
PZ7.W3876Yan 2009
[Fic]—dc22   2008011229

ISBN 978-1-58246-431-2 (PJ Library)

Design by Chloe Rawlins
Typeset in Adobe Garamond Pro, Copperplate Gothic, Juergen,
Michaelmas, and Oldstyle.
The illustrations in this book were rendered in oils.

MANUFACTURED IN CHINA

031930.2K2/B1356/A8

To my family:
to Eli, and to the kids—Rachel, Menachem, Yitzchak, Hadassah, and Malka.
You make stories worth telling and memories worth keeping.
—EW

For Sam.
—AG

It was all over.

On the day before Passover, with Mother busy supervising the cook, with potatoes boiling and apples stewing and beef bubbling in carrot-studded gravy, General Robert E. Lee surrendered. There were still some troops fighting outside Virginia, but my father said it didn't matter. The war was really over.

The War of Northern Aggression had started when I was seven. Now I was already ten and the Rebel Confederates had lost to the Union. I was never going to be a Rebel general. I'd never capture a whole unit of Yankees single-handed.

But war or no war, Passover is still Passover. My mother had been getting ready for months. The whole house had been scrubbed clean from the attic to the cellar, just to make sure we didn't own a single bit of bread. If a stray crumb did somehow find its way into our house, it would just die of loneliness.

Grandpapa took down the leather-bound Haggadahs from the highest shelf in the parlor. The Haggadahs, which explain the whole order of the seder, the festive Passover meal, were in large Hebrew letters, splotched with wine stains from years past. Every year at this time, we remember how the Jewish people were slaves in the land of Egypt long ago, and how we were led out of slavery and into freedom. We sing songs and eat special foods to remind us how bad it was to be slaves, and how good it is to be free. Of course, with the war these last four years, we've been talking about slavery for as long as I can remember.

Yesterday morning, when Father and I went to pick up our matzoh, I heard talk of rioting in Richmond and whispered worries of worthless Confederate money. No one knew whether the Union would treat us well, now that they'd beaten us. But word had spread that at least our soldiers would be allowed to take home their own horses to work their farms.

Yankee soldiers patrolled the streets, walking around as though they owned Virginia. To be fair, I guess they did own Virginia now.

I took a piece of matzoh and sat down on the front porch to settle my thoughts. Mother didn't approve of snacking between meals, usually, but the seder wouldn't start till after the stars came out, and the meal part doesn't happen till a good hour after that. Meanwhile, a boy's got to eat.

I was crunching my matzoh when a Yankee soldier, the real thing, came walking down the street. He was a corporal—I could tell from the yellow double chevrons on his sleeve.

A real, live Yankee, just walking up the street. The war might be over, but we were still plenty angry. I thought maybe I should take the barrel of rainwater at the side of the house and soak him.

I was still thinking of ways I could be brave when the Yankee opened our gate and stopped right in front of our porch. "Hello, young man. A good holiday to you! May I have some of that matzoh?"

If my eyes could have gotten wider, I'm sure they would have. I held my matzoh out with a trembling hand and watched as he took it gently and then ate it in one bite. I ran inside as fast as I could.

"Mother!" I hollered. "There's a . . . there's a . . . a Yankee Jew outside!"

My mother smoothed her dress, patted down her hair, and took my hand. She led me right back out to the porch. That Yankee was just standing there, waiting.

When he saw my mother, he bowed a little and said, "Ma'am, I'm Myer Levy. I hope I didn't frighten anyone. I just got leave for Passover and—"

"And you'll be having your seder with us tonight. We'll be pleased to have you, Mr. Levy. I'm Celia Josephson, and the young fellow who greeted you so memorably is my son Jacob. Mr. Josephson will be home shortly. Please come in."

And he did. Mother sent our housemaid, Nettie, to prepare him a room and told her to set an extra place at the table. Nettie found our Jewish customs a little odd, shaking her head often at our porkless kitchen, but seeing a Southern family hosting a Yankee in full uniform must have been too much for her. She actually laughed out loud before leading Corporal Levy upstairs to the guest room.

Mother told me to let our guest sleep until it was time for the seder.

"Mother," I whispered. "Mother, how could you let a Yankee into our house?"

"Jacob, every year we begin the seder the same way. We say, 'All who are hungry, let them come and eat; all who are in need, let them join us for the Passover meal.' A hungry man needing a seder has come to our home. Would you send him away for wearing a blue coat?"

Maybe.

About an hour later, the Yankee came out of his room in a fresh white shirt. He still wore his hat, and under it his hair was damp where he had washed his face. He had taken off his saber, too.

I followed him downstairs and watched as he introduced himself to my father and my grandfather. Corporal Levy held out his hand.

"Mr. Josephson, thank you for inviting me. You have a lovely home and a fine family."

My father thanked him. Then they sat down and looked at their feet. Now, I know that when three men sit in our front parlor, the only thing they're talking about is the war. So it was something to see as they all tried to make polite conversation without talking about the one subject that was most on their minds.

Grandpapa spoke first. "And where are your people from, Mr. Levy?"

"Philadelphia, sir. We've been in Philadelphia since the 1790s. And if I am not mistaken, sir, you are not originally from these parts."

Grandpapa laughed. His German accent was so heavy that even when he spoke English or read Hebrew, it still came out sounding like German. Of course he wasn't from these parts.

"No, indeed, I came from Bavaria as a young man. How I settled in Virginia is a long story, but I have come to love this place. My son and grandchildren were born here."

Just then, Mother appeared at the parlor door, the sign to come in to the dining room for the seder.

We always had a beautifully set table, but tonight the room almost glowed. Heavy clawfoot candlesticks that always put me in mind of dragon legs sat on the sideboard. All the silver had been scrubbed and polished for Passover. It looked like there were mirrors all over the room. My sister, Minna, had filled vases with bright pink and white azaleas clipped from our hedges. When he saw the table all laid out, our guest looked near ready to cry. He turned to my mother and said, "Mrs. Josephson, you've no idea how much a soldier appreciates a finely set table." I couldn't believe what he was saying. Me, I would be willing to give up the fancy table any day for a chance to eat over campfires.

My father looked up sharply. "We're among the lucky ones, to still have our house and supplies. Atlanta's burned and Richmond's ruined, you know." He opened his Haggadah to the first page, and the seder began.

"Levy, have you any Hebrew?" he growled at our guest. "Because if you do, we'll expect you to read along."

And he did. Corporal Levy knew all the words, better than my father and almost as well as my grandfather.

We got along fine until Minna asked the Four Questions and someone had to answer them. Why matzoh instead of bread? Why the bitter herbs? Why do we dip our vegetables and bitter herbs? And why are we leaning on pillows?

Grandpapa knew the answers to all the questions, and he began the story at the beginning. He answered in his German-Hebrew. "*Avodim hayinu*, we were slaves to Pharaoh in Egypt, but the Almighty One took us out of our bondage. Minna, Jacob, do you understand what this means?"

Father answered in our place. "Children, it means that no man needs to submit to the tyranny of an evil government. No one needs to be subject to a cruel ruler. Levy, wouldn't you agree that sometimes rebellion is a good thing?"

There were little beads of sweat making a mustache above our guest's upper lip. He swallowed hard. "Sir, it is one thing to rebel against an unjust government. But Passover isn't about people rebelling against a government, sir. It's about how no man wants to be a slave and about how wonderful it is to be free."

The room was very quiet. Minna crumbled matzoh between her fingers.

Grandpapa spoke up. "Gentlemen, haven't you noticed that the Haggadah is full of disagreements? That's part of the service. Now, let's keep on, or we'll never get to the meal."

We read about the Ten Plagues, and with each plague, poured a little wine from our glasses. Grandpapa said, "This reminds us that, even though the Egyptians had to be punished for their wickedness, we can't drink a full cup of wine or feel completely at ease with the victory, knowing that other people have suffered." He raised his eyebrows at Corporal Levy.

Levy smiled, "Absolutely correct, sir."

And so we plowed through plagues and praises until it was time to eat.

When Corporal Levy broke the matzoh into two pieces and hid the larger part to eat for the afikoman, the last part of the seder meal, I kept a careful eye. As soon as he got up to wash before the meal, I snatched the hidden matzoh from behind his chair.

Now I had Corporal Levy's afikoman, and he wouldn't be able to finish the seder without it. I was going to demand a good ransom from the Yankee. Most years, I stole Father's afikoman and Minna stole Grandpapa's, and we always got toys in exchange for handing over the matzoh: china dolls for Minna, little metal soldiers for me. This year, I was hoping for something better.

I was so busy considering what I wanted from Corporal Levy that I ate without tasting any of the food. We started with chicken soup and matzoh balls. Then we had beef with carrots and sweet potatoes, and for dessert, stewed apples with pecan pralines.

Late at night, when the long, tapered candles were beginning to sputter, it was finally time for the afikoman. Corporal Levy looked behind his chair. When he saw that his matzoh was missing, he turned to me.

"All right, young man, what'll it take for me to get that afikoman back?"

"Your saber, sir."

My father looked like he was holding back a laugh. Maybe it was just a sneeze.

Mother said she wouldn't be allowing any sabers in this house, so instead, Corporal Levy promised me his hat. With the war being over, he was sure he wouldn't need it any more.

"Now you can tell all your friends that you got a Yankee's head. Will that do?"

Maybe.

Corporal Levy headed back to his unit the next morning with a kerchief tied around his head. Mother packed him a basket of cold beef and matzoh and a dozen boiled eggs. We stood together on the porch as he walked off, watching his tall boots kick up little eddies of dust.

"Well, that was something, wasn't it?" she asked. I agreed that it was.

Even though the war was over, things didn't settle down for a long time. On the fifth night of Passover, an actor called Booth shot President Abraham Lincoln in a theater. People around here didn't miss Lincoln too much, but they were still shaken up by the shooting.

The next year, Passover was much harder. We had sold most of our land outside town and even a few pieces of silver. The picket fence was burned for firewood, the paint on the house was peeling, and the rhododendrons in the side yard had been cut down for kindling.

But we did have one nice surprise for that Passover. A week before the holiday, the post office received a barrel addressed to my father. Tied to the barrel was an envelope with a note inside. When we brought the barrel home, Father read the note aloud to us all.

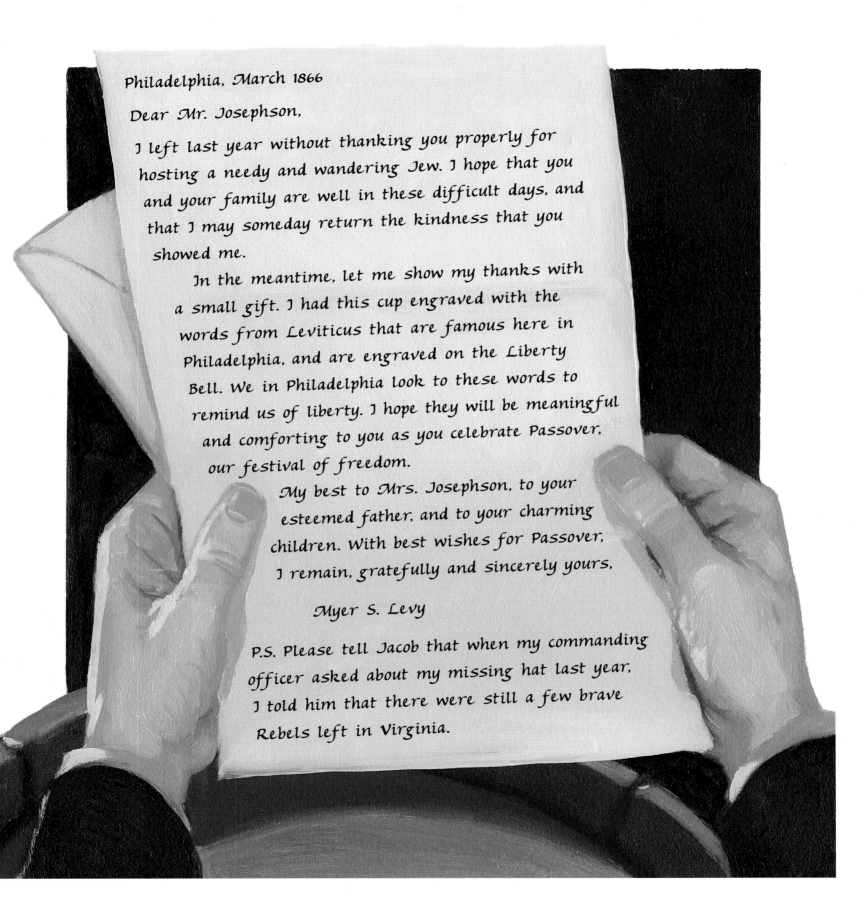

Philadelphia, March 1866

Dear Mr. Josephson,

I left last year without thanking you properly for hosting a needy and wandering Jew. I hope that you and your family are well in these difficult days, and that I may someday return the kindness that you showed me.

In the meantime, let me show my thanks with a small gift. I had this cup engraved with the words from Leviticus that are famous here in Philadelphia, and are engraved on the Liberty Bell. We in Philadelphia look to these words to remind us of liberty. I hope they will be meaningful and comforting to you as you celebrate Passover, our festival of freedom.

My best to Mrs. Josephson, to your esteemed father, and to your charming children. With best wishes for Passover, I remain, gratefully and sincerely yours,

Myer S. Levy

P.S. Please tell Jacob that when my commanding officer asked about my missing hat last year, I told him that there were still a few brave Rebels left in Virginia.

We pried open the barrel to find it filled with matzoh and a bottle of wine. At the very bottom was a silver goblet, inscribed in Hebrew.

PROCLAIM LIBERTY THROUGHOUT ALL THE LAND
UNTO ALL THE INHABITANTS THEREOF

I was still a brave Rebel, but Corporal Levy showed me that a truly brave soldier is a man who can win people's hearts.

Father and I began to help Mother scrub the house for the holiday. Passover was just ahead, and the war was behind us now.

The Real Story

This story takes place at the very end of the American Civil War, which was fought from 1861 to 1865. The war was fought between the United States (also called the Union or the Northern states) and the Confederate States (referred to as the South and made up of eleven states). To Southerners who felt justified in their cause, the war was known as the War of Northern Aggression. One of the reasons the Southern states broke away, or seceded, from the United States was because they believed each state should have the right to decide for itself whether to allow slavery. The United States, under the leadership of President Lincoln, wanted to limit slavery and eventually get rid of it completely.

It was a long and difficult war. More than six hundred thousand soldiers died and many more were wounded. On April 9, 1865, Confederate general Robert E. Lee surrendered to Union general Ulysses S. Grant to end the war and bring the South back into the United States. During the war, six thousand to nine thousand Jews fought for the North and about two thousand Jews fought for the South. Nearly one-third of all adult Jewish men in America fought in the Civil War.

There was a Jewish Union corporal (Fifth Regiment of the Cavalry, Company C) from

Photograph of Myer Levy's parents, Joseph and Rachel.

Philadelphia named Myer Samuel Levy, who found himself in a Virginia town for Passover. He saw a boy eating matzoh outside a house. When Levy asked for some of the matzoh, the child turned, ran inside, and yelled, "Mother, there's a Yankee Jew outside!" The mother promptly invited Levy in to eat with them that evening.

Myer Levy told the story to his family. His niece, Miss Miriam E. Levy, wrote a letter about it to historian Bertram Korn, who included it in his book, *American Jewry and the Civil War* (Jewish Publication Society, 1951).

Myer Levy was born September 12, 1839. His grandfather Aaron Levy Jr. came to Philadelphia in 1796. Myer Levy was the fourth of five children. He had three brothers, Moses, Elias Phineas, and Benjamin Franklin (no, not the famous one!) and a sister, Rebecca Virginia. After the Civil War, he returned to Philadelphia, married Sarah Jane Southwall, and together they raised ten children. He died April 8, 1909, at the age of 69, and is buried in the Mikveh Israel Cemetery in Philadelphia.

The Civil War did end right before Passover, and Lincoln was assassinated on the fifth night of the weeklong holiday.

During the period following the war, the South suffered through difficult economic times. Many Jews in the North, like the character of Myer Levy in this story, raised money to send Passover supplies to newly impoverished Jews in the South.

Believed to be Myer Levy and his wife, Sarah, in the early 1900s.

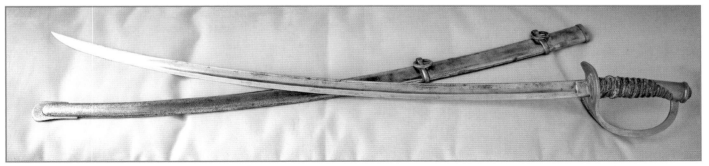

Myer Levy's saber, photographed especially for this book by Jason Wagner, son-in-law of Myer Levy's great-granddaughter, Judith McLaughlin.

Passover, the Festival of Freedom

When I first read the story about Myer Levy, I thought to myself that it must have been a very awkward holiday meal that night in Virginia. How could a Southern family host a Union soldier? But I also thought about how much Myer Levy must have had in common with his hosts. They were celebrating the same holiday, after all. And, of course, it wasn't just any holiday—it was Passover, the Jewish festival of freedom from slavery. It had some of the very same themes as the Civil War itself.

Passover commemorates the end of Jewish enslavement in Egypt and the birth of the Jewish nation. The holiday begins with the seder, an elaborate ceremonial meal that includes retelling the story of Passover, as it has been written down in the Haggadah. Some of the story is told in question and answer form, as in the recital of the Four Questions, to encourage the participation of children.

The seder also includes symbols of slavery and freedom. For example, bitter herbs and salt water at the table represent the bitterness and tears of slavery. The flat unleavened matzoh represents the poor food of slavery and serves as a reminder that the Jews left Egypt so quickly that their bread didn't even have time to rise. Leaning on pillows and drinking wine, on the other hand, are ways of expressing and celebrating freedom.

Matzoh is central to the Passover story—so central that breads and other leavened foods are forbidden throughout Passover. In many households, every room in the house is scrubbed, all

Pages from a nineteenth-century American Haggadah.

leaven is removed for the week, and different sets of both dishes and silverware are used for the holiday. At the end of Passover, the special tableware is put away and families go back to eating their regular foods.

The Yankee at the Seder is about people who found a way to overlook their differences and celebrate the things they had in common. That's not always an easy thing to do. I hope that this book makes it a little easier to focus on the things that unite us, and not on the things that divide us.

I wish you all the chance to share your holidays with loved ones, in harmony and peace.   —EW